SUPER SEMA

Meet the Technovators!

adapted by Terrance Crawford

PENGUIN YOUNG READERS LICENSES
An imprint of Penguin Random House LLC, New York

First published in the United States of America by Penguin Young Readers Licenses, an imprint of Penguin Random House LLC, New York, 2023

Super Sema™ and associated characters, trademarks, and design elements are owned and licensed by Kukua Education Limited.
© 2023 Kukua Education Limited. All Rights Reserved.

Visit us online at penguinrandomhouse.com.

Manufactured in China

ISBN 9780593659687

10 9 8 7 6 5 4 3 2 1 HH

Hi! I'm Sema! I may only be ten years old, but I'm already a maker, a creator, and a **super technovator**! That means I use my imagination, determination, and a helping hand from the amazing worlds of science and technology to solve problems and create really cool stuff!

Let's make! Let's create! It's time to technovate!

It's amazing what adventures **STEAM**—that's science, technology, engineering, arts, and math—can take you on!

 In Swahili, Sema means to express yourself, speak out, and talk!

This is my twin brother, MB. He's a tech genius who can code, decode, and reprogram anything!

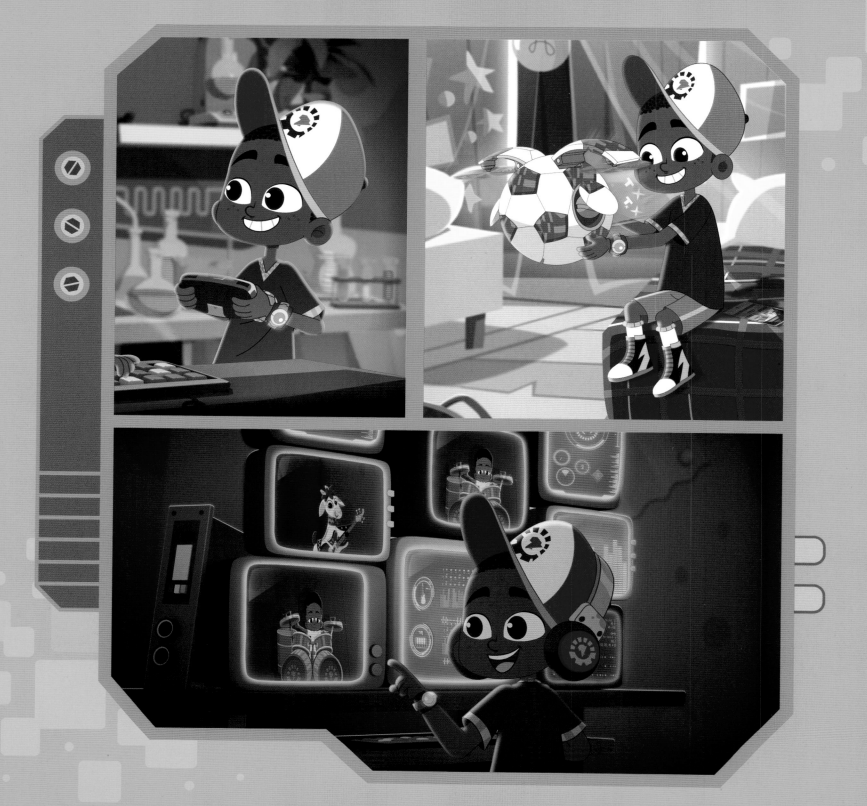

MB loves soccer more than saving the world, but he's a good sport and never makes me face the evil robot Tobor by myself. I don't know what I'd do without my brother!

MB's full name is Mwangi Baraka, but to me MB stands for MegaByte!

MB and I have lots of gadgets that we use on our adventures. My favorite is my **Uber-Nini**. It looks like a cool bracelet, but it's really a minicomputer!

I can use it as a walkie-talkie to talk to MB no matter where I am.

It also doubles as an interactive projector that lets me work on my technovations in my lab or on the go!

MB's go-to gadget is REF, a voice-activated robot shaped like—what else?—a soccer ball! REF is a flying, talking, portable tech station that MB technovated from recycled materials in our lab, and he joins us on many of our adventures.

REF has Wi-Fi, GPS, voice recognition, cameras, transmitters, and nanoparticles—which can be smaller than some wavelengths of light!

A technovation is a cool new invention, or innovation, made using technology and other STEAM skills. You can technovate at home just like I do in my lab!

And this is who we're up against—**Tobor**. Tobor is an artificially intelligent (A.I.) being who looks like a human, but he's actually a robot. And he doesn't like humans very much! He thinks he's smarter and better than us and is always looking for a way to take over the world and make our lives miserable.

Tobor lives in a high-tech palace up on a hill overlooking Dunia, where he thinks up evil schemes with his army of pesky robots, the **Bongolalas**. Secretly, I think he's really just unhappy because he doesn't have a heart (Literally! There's no heart in his robotic chest!) and he takes it out on all of us. But I won't let A.I. triumph forever!

Tobor's name is the word *robot* spelled backward!

Tobor created the Bongolalas to help him carry out his evil plans, but they seem to just mess things up for him more often than not! These little blue robots cause lots of mischief and mayhem wherever they go, but not always on purpose.

They are so energetic and curious about the human world that I think the bungling Bongolalas can't help but get themselves into all sorts of trouble. I love seeing the Bongolalas imitate humans—drinking cups of tea, baking **mandazi**, playing with slime, and, more than anything, throwing dance parties—which makes them laugh and drives Tobor crazy!

Mandazi is a small, sweet cake of fried dough.

When Tobor has to go somewhere on one of his evil missions, he usually leaves three Bongolalas called Hardware, Bluetooth, and Cookie in charge.

Hardware is the leader of the Bongolalas and is a bit of a bully. He almost always sends the other Bongolalas to do Tobor's dirtiest jobs, so underneath that strong robotic exterior, I think he's actually really just scared! Hardware's antlers are cool—they spin around like propellers so he can fly. But I don't think he has a very good sense of direction, because he's always bumping into things!

Bluetooth is the communicator of the bunch, in charge of relaying Tobor's orders to the rest of the Bongolalas. But I think perhaps he has a wire disconnected somewhere, because he never gets Tobor's messages quite right! He loves Peter Pizza's delicious pies and Mrs. Tam-Tam's sweet mandazi treats and will do anything to get his robotic hands on them!

Now **Cookie** is different. She's eager to please, sweet, and ever-so-slightly smitten with human beings—and Tobor's not so happy about that! But we can't turn away her enthusiastic, smiling face, and Cookie knows she's always welcome in our home.

Bongolala translates to "sleepyheads" in Swahili.

MB and I live with our grandpa **Babu**. Babu is old and wise and a fantastic storyteller with the energy of a kid like me!

Babu didn't grow up with technology and doesn't always understand my technovations, but he loves and supports me no matter what I do—and I've caught him curiously pushing buttons in my lab more than once!

Babu is the Swahili word for "grandfather"!

Moyo is our adorable pet goat we adopted when he was a baby. Even though he will eat just about anything, Moyo is as loyal as he is loveable, and we can't imagine our adventures without him. More than once, Moyo himself has actually saved the day!

Moyo **means "heart" in Swahili, which sums Moyo up. All heart, no head!**

Whenever I feel overwhelmed or doubt myself, I talk to **Mama Dunia**. A huge **acacia** tree in the middle of the town square, Mama Dunia is everything to us here in the village.

She gives us shelter from the sun, provides the air that we breathe, and inspires me when I need her. Mama Dunia is the loving spirit that keeps us all happy and healthy and gives me the confidence to carry on and technovate to save the day!

Acacias are strong, weather-resistant trees that are native to regions of the world like Africa and Australia, where they are called "wattle trees"!

Aziza is my best friend and one of the most creative people I know. She absolutely loves music and art! Aziza isn't so sure about science, but that doesn't stop her from lending a hand whenever we need one—and she always makes our technovations better. I think that a little encouragement is all Aziza needs to harness the power of STEAM in her own fun and creative way!

Noah is the youngest one in the group, and he has a big, big imagination! Noah is constantly dreaming up fantastic ideas like a bouncy bed made of bubblegum or a jelly-bean machine!

Even though he's little and sometimes a bit unsure of himself, Noah is a fantastic technovator. After all, every kid has the power to change the world!

All good inventions come from inspiration, determination, and a bit of technovation, but it helps to have a special place where you can practice your STEAM skills. That's why I'm grateful for my lab, where I can technovate with my friends and family!

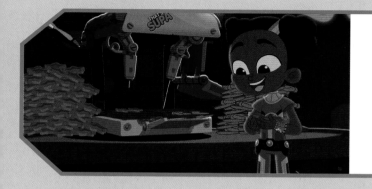

Here at the **print station**, I use 3D print technology to bring my ideas to life!

A big part of technovation is learning your way around a **computer** like the massive one I have in my lab!

If the journey of a thousand miles starts with one step, then all of my inventions begin here, with a **sketch**!

Sema and her friends always use their safety equipment when practicing STEAM!

Our lab has everything we need to technovate cool new apps, print 3D pizzas, engineer rockets, and anything else we dream up!

Many of Sema and MB's inventions are made from recycled material. That's good for the earth and just plain cool!

Science and technology are their own kind of superpowers! Have you ever created energy from garbage? Or had a snowball fight in the middle of a superhot day in Africa? I have! If you can dream it, you can achieve it, all thanks to the power of STEAM.

Besides being fun and interesting, STEAM helps us ask questions, connect dots, think creatively, and be innovative. Whether you're solving a problem or saving Dunia, there's no telling what STEAM can do for you!

We don't all have superpowers, but with a little love, we can all make the world a better place. If you ever find yourself in a bind, just remember that you already have the perfect way to solve a problem: Break down the big problem into little problems and deal with them one by one! You just have to use a little bit of logic and a lot of creativity. Then you stand tall and strong, open your arms, and say . . .

"Let's Technovate!"

Time to show the world what **every** kid can do!